MW00941731

GOD

DEATH

START

a dream
by Steven Rouk

GOD

DEATH

START

a dream
by Steven Rouk

I had a dream last night about a book
that was written by a friend
and passed from person to person around me.
I was curious,
I was jealous,
I was excited,
but I did not read the book.
When I awoke, I decided to write it.

What follows is the inspiration from that dream,
a vivid hallucination-inspired fury of words
detailing various aspects of existence and nonexistence
as seen through the mental lens
of a twenty-something-year-old.
And, just as in the dream,
this fury will be called

G O D   D E A T H   S T A R T

a dream

by Steven Rouk

GOD DEATH START

About the Author

Steven Rouk is the author of many award-winning novels that have yet to be published, or even finished. He holds a degree in Mathematics from Arizona State University and spent four years pursuing music with the band While We're Up and as a solo artist under the name Steven Mitchell Rouk. He currently lives and breathes in Colorado where he turns information into visually digestible images, as well as actively working to end the brutalization of other-species creatures.

He would like to inform you that this book may be offensive to some readers, but not nearly as offensive as the actual injustices present in our everyday lives, so he asks that you please focus on helping correct those instead of getting too worked up about some creatively placed words on a page. If you would like a list of said injustices, he would be more than happy to oblige.

Oh, and he also wishes you "nothing but the best and most fulfilling life possible, my dearest friend."

Thr	*sixsix*	*sixsix*	*neninenin*
.	*wo*	*inenineni*	*tw*
o	*sixsix*	*hre*	*ree*
four	*four*	*neninenin*	
n	*ree*	*eninenine*	*sevense*
fivef	*thr*	*eth*	*hteighte*
nineninen	*ighteigh*	*evensev*	*e*
tw	*eet*	*fivef*	*sixsix*
sixsix	*tw*	*n*	*four*
ivefi	*venseve*		
eet	*eninenine*	*ivefi*	*sixsix*
vefiv	*efive*	*eighteig*	*ot*
eighteig		*wo*	*ighteigh*
inenineni	*ot*		*sixsix*
sevense	*teightei*	*nineninen*	*wo*
neninenin	*ghteight*	*enseven*	
hre	*four*	*four*	*teightei*
ot	*e*	*inenineni*	*eninenine*
eth	*nineninen*	*four*	*nineninen*
hteighte	*nsevens*	*four*	*ghteight*
four	*o*	*vefiv*	*sixsix*

I've been a cyclist long enough to know that it's a good day

any day I don't get hit by a car.

PART I

Thomas Shermer dies at 8:01 AM on December 3rd.

At 8:02 AM, Thomas Shermer is sitting in a burgundy high-back cloth chair, left leg crossed over the right in stiff khaki pants, his hands gently folded on his lap, in a dim wooden-ornamented room with a warm orange fire burning on the stone hearth in the opposite wall. In front of him is a small wooden table made from exquisite dark cherry wood, and on top of that a chiseled marble chess set. A clean-shaven wiry middle-aged man is staring at him with big brown eyes, a smirk on his face. Thomas looks up at him.

"Tom Shermer, welcome to heaven. A game of chess, Tom?" The man chuckles softly to himself, eyes kept on Thomas.

"Goodness…" Thomas says. He looks around the room. A large window to his right shows a near-impenetrable darkness except for small points of white light far off in the distance. Too far away, in fact. He blinks and rubs his eyes. "I'm not entirely sure…"

"You're in heaven, Tom. Now let's play chess," the middle-aged man with sunken cheekbones says rather abruptly, his smirk gone. "I want to play chess. I'm white, so I'll go first."

Thomas uncrosses his legs, looks again at the man, the man with the pure white shirt and golden tie, crisp black suit jacket to complement it all. The man with the comb-over, several hairs out of place.

"Alright, ok, I'll play."

The man moves a knight, and Thomas moves a knight up to match. In life, he had been a professional chess player for several decades and continued playing into his old age with friends and children who would oblige him. He had played a game with his grandson the day before his recent death, in fact.

The middle-aged man responds with a pawn, then curtly says "your move". Thomas moves a knight, the man a bishop. Pawn, castle, bishop, pawn up to meet another pawn. Thomas stops and looks at the man.

"Alright, who are you? Where am I?"

"Heaven, Tom. I told you you're in heaven." The man makes another move, his queen diagonally out to Tom's right, outside the safety of the pawns' barrier.

"It's just…but, I'm not sure —"

"You died, you're in heaven, I'm God. We're playing chess. It always takes so long for people to understand this," the man says, sighing an exasperated breath of air and leaning back in his chair with his eyes cast upward. His eyes shoot down to meet Thomas's. "Let's just play chess for now, shall we? No more questions." And he sits up again.

P A R T   I

GOD

1 And it happened in those days that 217 women throughout all the lands joined egg and seed in their wombs in the same moment, all unknown to each other, with many of the lands separated from each other by vast deserts, mountains, and oceans. [2]Each pregnancy is marked by the sudden transformation of the woman into a calm and healthful state, such that the people are made to wonder what is so special about these pregnancies. [3]Each woman lives in the loving continued union with a partner, man and woman existing together in harmony. [4]Nine months later, on exactly the same day in the early months of the year, all of the women give birth without complications. [5]Thus, on that day 217 new humans of every race and creed enter the world, both male and female, 108 girls and 107 boys. [6]The babies are utterly calm even as they are born, and they cry very little throughout their childhoods.

[7]Because of the mysterious nature of the transformation of the mothers and the peaceful babies, the children grow up in the council of the wisest and most compassionate of the communities, and they learn even more how to be calm and slow to anger or judgment. [8]Some even say the children are wise, while others exclaim "How can a child possibly be wise! They are so young and inexperienced in the tragedies of life." [9]The communities know these children are special, although as of yet they are unaware of the existence of the other 216 children elsewhere around the globe.

[10]The children grow into young adults under the guidance of the villages and towns, and it is known that they are intelligent and understanding much beyond their years. [11]Their compassion is unmatched, they find favor with everyone they meet, and no one is able to hate them or hold grudges against them. [12]Everything they say can be trusted completely, because it is known they are among the most truthful in the land.

2 On the 17th anniversary of their births, the 217 young men and women gather their communities together to make an announcement. Everyone shows up to hear them speak. [2]"There are others, like me," they say. "There are others who are me, and I am them. We have come to every region of the globe to aid you in the trials of life and living. You are loved, and we are here to give you life as you have never known. But," they say, "there is much work to be done."

[3]The people are excited beyond belief and are compelled to action immediately. [4]The people say "What do they mean when they said others? What others are there, and how can they all be the same?" [5]The communities send delegates to other lands in every far-reaching part of the earth, and on the way they discover exactly the same thing. Every other place has also sent out delegates to determine the truth of what these young men and women have said. [6]Messengers meet each other on paths in-between towns, each of them running quickly, and when they spot the other they exchange words of greeting and then embrace the other upon hearing the good news. [7]Joy overtakes each nation, although each person is filled with much mystery and curiosity. [8]The people have no idea what is happening, but it fills them with wonder.

[9]The young men and women perform miracles for the next several years. These great acts are not physical miracles or scientific miracles, but human miracles. [10]The young people say "Your lives will be improved by more than you can imagine if you can work together on this," and immediately the townsfolk gather to combine their efforts on the project. [11]With the guidance of the young adults, the people follow through, and everything happens perfectly. [12]Every time that the people of a community are compelled to work on a problem together, the problem is solved in a matter of days or weeks. [13]Soon, the effects of these efforts are undeniable. Everyone has enough food. Everyone has somewhere to sleep.

[14]"This is just the beginning," the adults say, with the number of their years now increased to twenty-five, then twenty-six, then twenty-seven. [15]"The joy you feel now is nothing compared with what's

coming. Let me show you," they say. [16]The years pass exuberantly and the holidays are filled with celebration. Every community has been transformed in the best and most unimaginable of ways, with every impossibility becoming a reality. [17]Every city, every nation, has improved to the point of being unrecognizable to their former selves. [18]Truly, some of the older in the community say to each other, "How is it that our lives are so different from when we were young? Before, we used to reminisce about the past, and now we enjoy the present and anticipate the future with glowing hearts."

[19]After more years pass, the miracle-workers no longer tell people what to do; instead, the 217 work collaboratively as co-leaders with many others in the communities, making decisions as a group. [20]Other people begin to take the lead, guided to wisdom by the collective love and instruction of the communities, and these new leaders are given full support by the people. [21]Yet, even with this much time having passed, none of the 217 has ever seen another one. In fact, none has ever left the community into which they were born, although each seems to have great knowledge of the entire world.

3 Time goes on, and the world is united. Each community now puts the needs of everyone above the wants of the few, and the nations slowly learn that all other communities have been transformed in similar ways as themselves. [2]The commonalities make it nearly effortless for the different peoples in distant lands to work together and to trade their goods with each other. [3]Suffering has become a rarity, and even death has no sting. Love is unbounded and everywhere.

[4]The mysterious 217 age with the years, growing old and seldom taking the role of leader in their communities anymore. Instead, they spend their time playing with the children and telling them wonderful stories that teach the young ones about love and how to treat all creatures with respect and kindness. [5]They spend time each week helping the communities grow food from the earth and cooking that produce for the people. [6]Sometimes they watch the wild creatures of nature, smiling at them knowingly.

[7]After 70 years of life had been lived since their births, all 217 old men and women die on the same day, admired and loved. [8]People throughout every land mourn and erect monuments, but they are filled with joy knowing they are forever changed. [9]"Never will the world forget the 217," they say. "Oh, how beautifully they gave their lives to us all! Never will we forget their boundless expression of love for us."

DEATH

When I was on the road, I primarily learned one thing. If god exists, then it's in the extreme kindness shown by my fellow human beings. If the devil exists, he too is composed of human thoughts and actions.

Indeed, we are the holiest and vilest of existence. Better and worse than anything we could dream up.

Traveling the country as a sort-of-professional-musician was my career for a while. I call it a career because it implies less income than "job" does, perhaps, although I did make enough to feed myself for a while. *(Citation: I'm still alive at the time of writing this.)*

My main mode of transportation was an old van that used to go by the name The Golden Bullet. That van was a powerhouse, let me tell you. It had nearly two hundred thousand miles on it when I started my musical trekking, and then I drove it clear around the country with little more than an oil change and a tire kick before leaving. That van and I put in 12,000 miles in just a couple of months, non-stop from city to city. I slept it in, I ate in it, I changed in it. Everything that normal humans have homes for, I had that van.

Woke up drenched with sweat from the heat of the sun every morning around 6:00 AM. Ate some meals of lukewarm beans straight from the can. Living the dream never tasted so good.

Of course, pushing anything that hard for that long is going to cause something to go wrong. In addition to a couple of flat tires that were easy enough to fix, I found myself in an empire-state-sized pickle when my van's starter completely died at a closed Bank of America on Staten Island when I didn't have enough money to even cross the toll bridge off of the island. I was broke, completely broke, and stranded in a place I knew practically nothing about. To say I was living off of credit at this point in my life would be a massive understatement. I was clinging on to my thread of an existence with some debt and the help of strangers.

My starter died, I needed around half a grand to fix it, and the repairs couldn't even be completed in one day. I would end up scraping together the money with a little help and continuing on my merry way (spoiler alert), but the story begins with me not having a place to sleep for the night. See, my van truly was my home — can't get better than a free four-wheeled motel anywhere there's a parking lot. So while my van was in the shop, I was bedless.

And this, ladies and gentlemen, is how I ended up at a McDonald's (desperation is how anyone ends up at that god-forsaken place) frantically using my phone to search for cheap hotels, cheap hostels, homeless shelters, really anywhere that would take me for the night. I'd never been in New York, and I was broke and scared. It was one of the most intense moments of my life, wondering what in Dante's 7th Circle was I doing trying to be a touring musician as my career. I was a kitten in a dog park.

I found a dormitory-style communal hostel for $30 a night in Chinatown, downtown Manhattan, and I thought I could scrape together that much money as long as I had a few good days of CD sales coming up. So I went over to a table where a Jamaican mother and her daughter were doing some work — the daughter was studying for the SAT, and the mother was working on papers for her job — and I asked them which way the ferry to Manhattan was and whether or not it was truly free, since I couldn't really afford to be mistaken. Yes it was free, they said, and then the mother asked me what on earth I was doing trying to walk two miles in the evening to a ferry with a bag full of clothes and looking like some pop-punk boy-band wanna-be with my cut-off jean shorts, tank top, and bracelets. Which is exactly what I was. (Still am a little, depending on the day.)

Well madame, I said, I'm obviously not the brightest candle in the chandelier, just here trying to make a living by selling my music to teenagers who don't know better. Say hello to the embodiment of what you encourage your children not to be.

I didn't say that. After describing my broken-down van situation, the unthinkable and miraculous happened. She simply invited me to stay with them for the night. To sleep in their guest room, to eat a delicious vegetarian Jamaican dinner with them, and to ride back with them to the car shop the next morning to see about my car. Me, the dirty vagabondish stranger they had just met in a fast food joint.

I accepted with a glad heart, but I was also weary from being so low and unable to provide anything back to them. I decided to try my best to return the favor with some conversation and smiles, and to this day I hope that they considered it worthwhile to house me for the night.

This is the miracle of human beings, ladies and gentlemen. If you don't believe in love, lose everything. It comes flowing from the cracks in your life to fill you back up and repair your broken spirit.

If you don't believe in love, lose everything.

START

People sometimes talk about the future, the present, and the past as if they were homogenous substances that can be described with some simple adjectives like "better", "technological", "fatter". But right now as you read this, there are millions and billions and trillions of different worlds on our planet, trillions of ways of living life. We don't need to look into the future or past to find strange and wonderful things. We need only look in the present.

These things could happen anywhere. They could be happening now on earth, or perhaps on another planet.

If they're not happening where you are, then you can create them. But before you can create, the first thing you must do is start. And to start, you must imagine.

Here are some visions.

...

Hate and anger are the first two things you learn to control in this world. Before math, before history, even before language people are taught to control their emotions, especially the negative ones. The introspective arts have had a large role in this — introspection, meditation, and exercise as well — since they have been shown to reduce negativity.

When children first show the signs of anger or hatred, they are swept away by a teacher who helps instruct them in the handling of these emotions.

Breathe. Move your arms. Close your eyes. Picture yourself flying above, in the clouds, then space. You're in nature. Now let's walk. Together, you and I.

The children learn to befriend these feelings, to look on them kindly and then transform them into helpful internal emotions, which translate into compassionate and respectful external actions. With this one change, fractures in society are slowly healed, politics has become overwhelmingly more effective than ever before through meaningful dialogue, the overall intellect has soared, and crime has practically vanished.

Some people don't go on to learn the sciences, or math, or history, or art. Many do. But all live together peacefully, because that is the first and foremost thing that they have learned to do.

...

In this world, food is provided to you by prescription. You don't have a choice of what to eat, and many people find it a strange concept that at one point in time others did have a choice. Choices, they say, could very well lend one to become unhealthy, and health is by far the greatest wealth without which everything else is meaningless. Why would we allow personal choices to potentially damage our well-being?

Doctors prescribe exactly the diet that each person needs based on their specific unique physiology. If a person desires a change in diet, they consult their doctor who ultimately has the right to agree and prescribe the change or not. People understand either way with no hard feelings because there is a great deal of trust in the medical-nutritional system.

As a result of this system, good health is practically universal and disease is a rarity. People enjoy long, healthy lives full of good food and exercise. They also enjoy their jobs more because of the psychological benefits of good health combined with the good-natured temperaments of their co-workers and supervisors. When sickness and hard times do come, people are much more equipped to handle these things. With a majority healthy population, the web of humanity is made exponentially stronger and the positive effects are felt in everything.

...

P A R T   I

In this world, society is more and more choosing to live in co-ops: large cooperative housing complexes where dozens of people live together, sometimes with their families. These establishments often grow their own food, make their own clothes, and have regular meetings to discuss how much energy their household consumes and how many resources they use. They assume as harmonious a relationship with nature and with their community as they can.

...

In this world, one person is chosen for the mission to Mars. It's quite expected that this person will never return and that they will be completely cut off from physical human interactions from the moment they step into the spacecraft to leave earth.

No one is sure who will want to step forward. Will anyone who chooses to go be mentally hardy enough to actually do the mission? Is it not contrary to the definition of good mental health to actively choose eternal social deprivation? How will we know they won't lose their mind on the way?

Yet in time there is one woman who comes forward, an intelligent and gentle lady who is moderately introverted and well-liked by her peers. She understands what she is doing and has accepted that she will not return or encounter humans again. She has made peace with these things, and she gets tested for the journey by various psychologists who all say she is as mentally stable as anyone else to be found. Whether this turns out to be stable enough to survive the journey is yet to be seen, but time will tell.

She is allowed to bring a couple of personal items with her, weighing no more than two kilograms together and taking up very little space. She chooses the book A Tale of Two Cities by Charles Dickens, with a small picture tucked inside the front cover of her and a young girl.

The day of the launch comes, and there are many people who think she won't go through with the mission, that she will back out in the last moments and the whole thing will fail. But she doesn't — she climbs into the space capsule as planned, checks the launch consoles and runs through final departure lists with central command, then the countdown comes. As the final numbers are read off she says a few words silently to herself, and then the rockets fire. At that moment, she knows, humanity begins a new era of journeying into the deepness of space.

...

In this world, we become immortal. Cracking the biology of it turned out to be surprisingly simple, so simple that it is now an elementary exercise in college biology to construct an immortal gene replacement sequence. The difficult part ended up being the physics constraints — it was long believed that there was only so much useable energy in the universe, with everything ending in heat death and the universe ripping itself apart. The math is slightly too complex to list in these pages, but eventually a method of eternal energy sustainability was found. Even monstrous difficulties are eventually overcome by willful spirits and the cooperation of minds across generations.

Many also thought that humans couldn't psychologically bear being immortal. This turned how to be laughably false, and it was quickly seen how easily humans could deal with an endless life. Memory and neural connections may allow humans to remember a great number of things, but not an infinite. Colloquially speaking, we eventually start "weeding out" memories in order to free up brain power. Neuroscientists discovered that we do this kind of brain rewiring constantly in a lifetime, so a human life can be extended indefinitely with no detrimental psychological effects.

Humans also figured out long ago how to provide the essential needs and wants to everyone in society at a sustainable level, which means that immortality becomes nearly like heaven on earth. People are free to live out there lives with abundant time for friends, family, the arts, exercise, and nature.

...

In this world, we also become immortal. Unfortunately for this world, unlike how it could have been, society has neglected to solve some of the more elementary social issues that plague humanity. There are still people living on the streets, begging for money so that they can eat. The majority of society lives below the poverty line, and the money these people do make is typically spent on entertainment and pointless trinkets and decorations instead of on empowering themselves with investments in health and education. Exacerbating their poverty is the fact that almost 90% of this world is grossly overweight, even though the definitions for overweight and obese have been raised multiple times to account for the growing girth of the average citizen. The main culprits of this lack of health are massive food corporations who make a profit by providing addictive and unhealthy food at lower prices than real food. Citizens and governments are too scared or apathetic to regulate these detrimental food products, so the negative effects of these products snowball and impact every sector.

So although we now have the ability to live forever, in practice very few people can take advantage of that luxury because of the threat of violence and the restriction of the knowledge that leads to immortality. Many people attempt to lead large revolutions to obtain a high quality of life for everyone, but the people with the majority of the resources no longer have an interest in helping the vast legions of sickly and poor, so society does not progress.

A few of those people in the upper crust of society hole themselves up in enormous mansions secured by small armies of guards, and there they live out hundreds and thousands of years with little company other than the people they hire to protect them. Some of them tire of their pointless day-to-day routines and eventually kill themselves.

. . .

$$p =$$

686

479766013

060971498190079

908139321726943530014

3305409394463459185543183397

656052122559640661454554977296 3113914

8085803712198799971664381257402 8291115057151

If I could sum up everything I've learned in my life into a few words,

it might be "Live and help live."

PART II

This middle-aged man annoyed Thomas, mostly because he had just recently died and simply wanted some peace, and also perhaps a little explanation of how one can die and then suddenly appear to be sitting in a high-back cloth chair playing chess with someone who calls himself God. This was not exactly what Thomas had imagined death being like, and he wasn't sure whether or not he could be upset about it. That might just be much too silly for the occasion.

Thomas was not used to silliness in his life, actually. His had not been a typical life, being a professional chess player and all, but it had not been silly either. He was used to long hours spent at work, little time for socializing or exercising, straight-forward conversations with business partners and family members. Not much play was to be had in Thomas Shermer's recently departed life.

Which is part of why this whole situation was so damn confusing and infuriating, because of the vast silliness of it. Who would have ever thought that someone could be peeved at the details of their death and afterlife? Blissful in heaven perhaps, or tortured in hell, but "peeved" was never a word that one would use when discussing emotions in the afterlife. Yet here he was, peeved as all get-out.

Thomas leans forward and moves his pawn forward and to the right, taking one of the man's pawns. Nothing spectacular yet, just the initial positioning of the pieces. But if there's one thing he knew about chess, it was that the spectacular things rest wholly on the unspectacular foundations of the game. Good games can rest on great beginnings, but spectacular games require the element of surprise. The man moves his queen to take Thomas's pawn, and Thomas notices the bags under the man's eyes and his sallow cheeks. The man smirks again as he takes the pawn, quite visibly pleased that he's taken another of Thomas's pieces.

"I've never played chess, you know. This is my first time. I usually don't bother with trifling human inventions like this, but I figured since you were purported to be somewhat decent at it I might dabble momentarily." Silence always rushed back in to fill the space left when the man stopped talking, an uncomfortable silence shared between people who truly have nothing to talk about. Thomas moves a pawn one little step forward toward the man's queen. The man moves one of his middle pawns forward two in a showy leap, and Thomas takes a moment to breathe calmly and stare off into the distance.

He notices a clock hung on the wall, off to the right of the fireplace. It is an intricately carved wooden pendulum clock with a small door on the front where Thomas can see the silver pendulum swinging back and forth behind a glass window. The clock face itself appears to be gold-plated, shimmering with an unearthly light, and that's when Thomas notices that there are no numbers around the outside of the clock. There are no hands either, not an hour hand or a minute hand or a second hand ticking off time. He stands up to go look at it.

"I watched some humans playing the game, read some books, it was obvious enough to grasp. Human things always are," the man says as Thomas walks over to the clock. The floor is perfectly waxed beneath his feet, and his shoes slide the slightest bit as he places foot in front of foot to make the least notice and leave the smallest trace of his having tread on the wooden floor of heaven.

The clock face is devoid of numbers and hands, Thomas confirms, but there is an enormous array of lines and shapes carved into the golden metal. He notices that the shimmering is not actually caused by the reflection of firelight, but that there are actually lights being traced up and down the lines carved into the surface, lights that glow and throb and shine. Sometimes the lines and carvings themselves morph into other lines and shapes, the whole mechanism pulsing with a strange musical tempo. "What in the world does this do...?" Thomas mutters quietly to himself.

God is suddenly next to Thomas. "You won't be able to understand this, Thomas. Time does not exist as you think it does. It does not flow as you think it does. There is truly no way for me to explain to you what is happening here."

Thomas grumbles, then moves toward the window. "I wasn't even going to ask you, you know." He reaches the window, and after a few moments his eyes adjust the slightest bit to the darkness outside. Millions of points of light come into view, and his mouth drops open. "Wow..."

God is beside him again. "That's what everyone says, in case you were wondering. But for some reason, any beauty always grows old to you. Humans stare out of that window for weeks on end when they arrive, but it always ends the same. They simply grow bored of it." God walks back to his chair by the chess table. "Boredom is what happens when you haven't realized the extent to which you don't know something, Thomas. Humans should never be bored. Now come, play chess."

GOD

At one of the pinnacles of my religious devotion, I took the expression "pray without ceasing" seriously. As in, I would walk the halls of my high school praying the entire time I wasn't talking with someone. I would pray when I wasn't doing schoolwork, and I would sure as hell try to pray during it too. (Especially during difficult exams.) This kind of prayer is unsustainable. It's fossil-fuel-powered prayer.

So eventually I slipped back into my old ways and re-started my journey of being a typical non-omniprayerful individual, but still immensely devoted to being an active Christian and still potentially wanting to be involved in ministry. Then there was a slow transition that occurred during a couple of years in my life, a transition where small incongruities in my beliefs made themselves known to my mind. I thought about why there's evil in the world. I wondered about the timing and details of my messiah's life, and the fates of non-believing humans in other cultures. I considered the place of animals in our lives and grew to find the idea of sacrifice abhorrent. Then, in one of the most significant shifts in my life, I had my worldview rocked by the eventual understanding and acceptance of evolution, an idea that I had denied for years because of influence from my church peers and mentors, as well as the scriptures and beliefs that evolution seemed to contradict. The implications of evolution are far-reaching, and they provide a sharper lens through which one can view all of life in crisp daylight — a lens which radically enhanced and informed so many aspects of my worldview.

I considered devastating natural disasters, discrepancies in scripture, and many other inconsistencies and doubts that revealed themselves. In a furious flurry of all-nighters and endless consideration, I came to realize that a godless (or rather, Christian-God-less) world made the pieces fit together so much more tightly. Inconsistencies dissolved, loopholes snapped shut, and in a beautifully terrifying moment of cold air clarity I gave up my beliefs in order to build something different for myself, something vehemently opposed to my old worldview.

For a while, my newfound lack of beliefs defined me as I tried to reconstruct some semblance of purpose in my life. After a few more years of life and endless hours of reading and thinking had helped me develop a solid foundation again, I became less adamant about my lack of belief, less forceful about my rejection of religion and my opposition to those who believed. The emotion subsided, and pathos gave way to logos. In many ways, I became a new person twice over.

I can still be adamant and passionate about these things, but less so. I would say I've become less defined by my *lack* of beliefs and more defined by positive thoughts about the world, which is a very difficult transition to make when you're coming out of a lifelong religion. A consequence of this switch is that I've lost the evangelical streak of blood flowing through my veins — I have less of an impulse to convert or deconvert people, trying instead to simply listen to them, engage them. I have learned to believe in the power of diligent and respectful conversation, heavy on the side of listening, and to know the fantastic worth of unwaveringly seeking true understanding of every side of any discussion. Rather than staying in the port of the land I know best, I find it more useful to be like a boat adrift in the ocean, constantly learning how to use the stars to better find home.

It also helps to bring a sense of humor along.

(...and a towel.)

...

God is a beautiful idea. If I had an all-knowing best friend who could cure cancer and help me pass math exams, I'd probably worship them too. Then we get to have an eternal cuddle sesh in Heaven with all of my friends? Absolutely. Convert me now.

Divine inspiration and guidance would be a god-send (pun obviously intended) for nearly everyone in every situation ever. Over 300 million Americans who suddenly knew what to do with their lives and had transcendent help? I know, right? That *would* be a miracle. In God we trust, because the people here still have a hard time learning to recycle.

The life of Jesus can also serve to uplift and encourage many a downtrodden soul. There's a reason — many reasons, actually, that the life of Jesus started a religious branch that grew to be the most popular religion in the world. Of course, not all of those reasons are admirable: the crusades (*covert or die*) and colonialism (*Christianizing the savages*), case in point. But many of the teachings of Jesus are admirable. If there are nights in your life that you wouldn't have made it through without help from these teachings or the help of perceived supernatural assistance, then absolutely that is a wonderful thing for you, and I'm glad you could draw that kind of deep life-affirming inspiration.

(Note: This is assuming that human lives have positive worth in the world, an assertion that is legitimately questionable in this day and age because of the vast negative influence we have as a species. Perhaps we all have a net negative worth and would be better off not existing. Nevertheless, here we are. Not many people are willing to go bury themselves because of a utilitarian-based argument about their worth, myself included. They're much more likely to get very angry and not speak to you much after that.)

There are some difficulties with God, though — modern-day Christianity is what I'll be referring to here, since that's what is most popular and what I have the most experience with — and as much as I would love for there to be a supernatural prayer-answering best-friend cuddle-buddy, I just don't think Christianity has it right. Besides the eternally-ever-ongoing philosophical debates about the problems of supernatural omniscient omnipotent beings or non-beings, there are other problems of more emotive concern. Some examples.

Jesus said to love your enemy and pray for those who persecute you. (Matthew 5:44)

That's lovely; I think we could all use a little bit more of that in our lives.

God said he will dash sons and fathers against each other, and he will not pity nor spare nor have mercy, but will destroy them. (Jeremiah 13:14)

...Jesus, well that's rough. What about that love and praying thing?

Jesus said for the sinless to throw the first stone. (John 8:7)

Exactly! Compassion and understanding. I'm all on board.

God said people who curse their parents should be put to death. (Leviticus 20:9)

Alright, this God guy is more than a little insane, and he's spoiling the good thing that Jesus has going on here. This line in the Good Book would have most teenagers in the US executed, and then there would *really* be no one left to pay into Social Security. Hey Jesus, set this angry deity straight with one of your beautiful life lessons.

Jesus said whoever breaks even one of the smallest commandments in the Law will be called least in the kingdom of heaven. (Matthew 5:19)

Hmm...sorry parent-cursers, execution it is.

The mixed messages of love and condemnation that we find in ancient scriptures like the Bible are more than a little confusing if we take them as the word of God, although what's *more* confusing is reading the attempts of people who actually do try to reconcile these passages into their worldviews. It's absurd the elaborate justifications that people will create to try to logically weave together a cohesive story of a perfect holy book. Surely God could have had a little more clarity and consistency in writing his sacred commands and stories given that these messages have to be interpreted by human beings. Most of us have a hard enough time deciphering modern poetry or a text from someone a generation removed. How are we expected to understand the Bible? Yet again and again, people claim to glean absolute certainty about various metaphysical concepts from a set of texts that's thousands of years old and riddled with the oddities of our distant ancestors' cultures. Any time I want a good chuckle, I search the web for detailed descriptions of exactly what heaven looks like or the specific character traits of an omnipotent invisible deity that only cryptically interacts with the physical realm. People who probably couldn't explain how a radio works somehow seem to know intricate details of a supernatural realm that has been doubted by scores of intelligent people throughout all of history.

One of the primary troubles to be had with scriptures of any kind is this. In order to truly understand that some text is telling us the truth, shouldn't we have the mental capacity to digest and analyze that truth, to discover its truthiness? And, further, if we should have the ability to do that, shouldn't we also have the ability to simply discover and describe those truths for ourselves, from any source and any text? If these truths are meaningful truths instead of arbitrary, their existence should be discoverable in many multifaceted ways throughout the universe. Things that are good for humans and good for the planet should be objectively good in some discoverable, quantifiable way. To have the intellect to discover the truth in scripture is to have the intellect to not need the scripture.

(Haughty, I know. I am a sassy one.)

Consider this. What do we consider valuable in the lessons learned from a text like the Bible? Things that uplift us, that bring us joy, that keep us healthy, that help us interact with other human beings well, that help others, that help us learn true things about the world. Things of this sort, right? If someone tries defending hateful things from the Bible *("Do not have sexual relations with a man as one does with a woman; that is detestable." Leviticus 18:22)*, many Christians say they are reading it wrong. "That's not literal," or "That's just in there to show the historical context," or "The life of Jesus means we don't have to follow those rules anymore," or something like that. People typically reject texts that are contrary to their cultural norms and sensibilities and embrace ones that mesh well. Loving people reject hateful texts, but hateful people use them to justify terrible actions and gloss over the notions of temperance, compassion, and peace.

So then, could we not instead garner these life lessons from other sources without needing the rather hard-to-justify belief that the source is from an all-knowing and perfect something or someone? Pieces of truth can be gathered from the Tao Te Ching just as they can be read in the Bible. Love doesn't need a commandment to be good. Compassion doesn't need to be decreed from above. These things are good because they are good for us and others. That is all we need. And the discovery of these goods is more readily accessible when we embrace open-minded curiosity and reject dogmatic authority.

Dogma can justify anything, even hatred and death.

Love and compassion can only uplift.

And if your love and compassion aren't uplifting, you're doing them wrong.

But perhaps the worst thing about taking sacred scriptures as the ultimate source of truth is the fact that it eliminates the possibility of discussion among different groups of people. There are very real foundations of our moral systems and philosophies of life that we could pull from in order to find common ground between opposing factions or ideologies. For instance, it is a pretty standard and obvious ethical consideration in our culture that one shouldn't torture their pets because those animals would suffer unnecessarily. That's a common moral foundation that most people share. I could then appeal to that moral consideration and argue that all creatures deserve this kind of consideration from humans, including cows and chickens and pigs and sheep. If a creature is in our care, we ought to treat them kindly and with love. We can dig even deeper and explore the reasons why *anything* deserves moral consideration, and what kind of actions are justifiable toward whom. This kind of ethical argument relies on universal similarities we have as human beings. All great moral philosophies rely on this kind of reasoning, reasoning that is defensible across time and culture, based on principles that are hard-coded into our humanity.

If, however, an appeal is made to scripture, then anyone participating in the discussion must adhere to the opinion that the scripture is correct. But since Christians, Muslims, non-theists, and people of many other types of beliefs can live together in harmony, doesn't it seem inherently flawed to think that any one scripture should be used as the basis of discussions between groups of people? Doesn't the existence of peace among diverse groups lend itself as evidence that there are deeper truths common to all of us on which we can base ethics and relationships? Truths that transcend personal and religious backgrounds?

It is these truths we must strive to find if we are to make progress.

DEATH

Falling asleep is like lying down to die each and every night. When I was a child, I had the hardest time falling asleep because I wanted to be aware of the inherently unknowable — I wanted to know exactly when my consciousness slipped into the state of unconsciousness, and what that felt like. I couldn't stand the thought of another day full of memories and experiences and thoughts and feelings, only to lie down and have no recollection of my body for eight hours until I gasped awake in the morning, terrified of the blackness I had just endured.

These thoughts of that unfeeling blackness haunted me so much that I would lie awake for hours, trying to fight the shutting down of my senses. Each time my vision would blur into a mental soup of drifting off, the fear would wake me up again, knowing that I had almost disappeared into the dark for another night of sleep. I listened to music for hours to keep my brain entertained and engaged. But inevitably it would happen after however long of fighting it, and the next morning I would jolt awake with the realization that I had failed again. In this way, sleep began to be a burden.

Caffeine and mental stimulation became close friends in my high school and college years, because then I didn't feel the sleep coming on. Hours could pass with my brain on fire from my favorite drugs of learning and creating and exploring, often plugged into the internet in the days when Google was still new and none of my friends had Facebook accounts. Then, late into the night, at a point of which I was only vaguely aware, I would collapse from exhaustion and gladly embrace a moment to rest my head. I look back on those days fondly as some of the best of my life.

Of course, the story of sleep is also the story of dreams. Vivid, surreal dreams, wonderful and terrifying. In fact, the vast majority of my dreams throughout my entire life have been nerve-wracking, nightmarish adventures through whole worlds that get created in my mind at night. Dreams where I am surely about to die, or dreams where I am constantly fearing for my life, or dreams where I have committed terrible atrocities, where I know I'm surely going to spend the rest of my life behind bars, hated by all, hated by myself.

Even the good dreams are not so much pleasant as they are simply not terrifying. In my mind, there is only a single dream that immediately comes to mind as being truly enjoyable — but I'm getting ahead of myself.

...

I'm in a restaurant, a place that feels like one of my favorite breakfast places to have biscuits and gravy with my mother, but it doesn't particularly look like it. The lights are off, it's nighttime, and there is no one else there. I'm sitting in a booth by myself with my favorite blanket, when suddenly I notice the hallway to the kitchen has started glowing and flickering red, like a massive fire is burning in the back room. The hallway runs in the direction that I'm facing, but it's over on the other side of the room so that I can't actually look down it — I can only see the flickering and the glowing of the red light on the walls, the inconsistent light intermittently showing the empty booths and bare walls of the restaurant I'm in. I cower down in the booth, trying to lie as close to the seat as I can, terrified of what I think might be down that hallway, of what might be coming out of it at any moment. I know deep down that the flames are fires from hell, and if the demons know I'm here they will drag me there with them. This is a recurring dream, and I never see or hear anything else. Just silence, just the distant flickering of the burning dark red light on the dim walls, and the terror as I try not to be seen or heard. At some point, I wake up.

...

An outer space asteroid labyrinth is the best way I can describe it. Perhaps it started as a video game, where I signed up to go in this gravity-less maze with my brothers, perhaps I just started there. The walls are tight and made of gray asteroid rock, with tunnels and tubes leading every direction. I see my brother once, but other than that it's just me floating around by myself, trying to navigate through an endless series of twists and turns in every direction all around me. I finally navigate my way out, and I'm on the surface of the asteroid now, with a little gravity to hold me down and flowing rock hills and cliffs everywhere. Suddenly, my brother comes flying over the top of me in a dune buggy, flipping over and moments later crashing into the

ground far away from me with a terrible noise. I know he's dead, and
then I wake up.

...

Back alleys, dirty trash-infested streets that are only a few feet wide,
dark buildings on either side. A ceiling above. I know that I've stabbed
my old English teacher, her body in a black garbage bag down at my
feet. If anyone ever finds out what I've done, I'll go to jail for the rest
of my life — I know this. My English teacher, then, is standing in front
of me, her body green and corpse-like. She is staring at me evilly,
judging me, leading me to my arrest. Her head is cocked down, her
eyes up at me, neck bent, hair stringy and clothes tattered. She won't let
me get away with it. People come around the corner of the alley, see
me but not her, but I know it's coming. It's only a matter of time before
I'm caught, and jail will be my home for the rest of my life. I make
peace with this, then wake up.

...

I'm in a warehouse with multiple floors arranged in a tiered fashion
with the lowest floor on one side and the highest floor on the other
side, friendly grays and a slight tinge of desaturated green in the hue of
the floor and walls, a waterfall of stairs leading from one side of the
building to the other. There are a lot of people there with me, lots of
children, and then a huge muscular man who I used to know. This man
starts getting angry, he gets angrier and angrier until he takes out a gun
and starts shooting at people. Water fills up the warehouse, running
down the stairs and filling up the bottom floor, boxes and tables
floating everywhere, bodies floating in the water. I submerge myself,

ducking back and forth around the man and trying to go up to a higher level. The water is surprisingly clear and blue. I'm scared of drowning and being underwater for too long, yet I don't feel my breath running out at all. I see a few children in front of me, and I grab them to help them up to high levels, putting them behind boxes and tables to block the bullets coming our way. One of them is a young girl in a pink dress. Another child is helping others too, but he is behind me and I can't tell if they make it to safety. We make it up to a higher level, the man is still on the lower level, and I wake up.

...

My body turns into a skyscraper, a huge towering building with other movable buildings that are my arms and legs. My eyes are large windows, and I am behind them looking out over my body. I see my hands being raised, my arms lifting up, and I wonder how this colossal structure can possibly lift itself. The color purple fascinates me.

...

I'm in a futuristic technological city, where long large glass and metal hallways connect different buildings. I'm walking through these large hallways, about as big as those in a high school, with many other people in tight-fitting, shining, black rubberized gear walking by me. I feel like I'm going down. Occasionally I look outside and see the dense cluster of towering buildings, a seemingly infinite span of skyscrapers stacked beside each other, dark metal and glass and rounded building shapes that are beautiful and inspiring. I reach the bottom floor of this hallway after ducking down through a low opening. Then, I'm outside and the buildings are all lighting up in sequence, creating a beautiful display. Bright colorful lasers shoot through the sky, and I'm in a car stopped in the middle of all of these buildings but no one seems to mind because the show is so wonderful. I wake up, wishing I could go back to see the colorful lights.

...

I'm in another large city, and I am powerful. I look over the buildings from the top of one, and in my hand is a laser that can cut through anything and that travels forever. I am in awe of the power I possess with this weapon, and I am tempted to use it in any way I can. I point it at a building, turn it on with the push of a button on its sleek metallic body, and move it and the beam to the side. The building is cut in half and begins a mammoth self-destruction, crumbling and collapsing to the ground. I destroy another building in the same manner, and another, then I simply wave the laser all around the city, slicing everything into pieces, watching it all crumble and fall into dust and debris. I fear for myself suddenly and find a stairwell, jumping down entire flights at a time and swinging from the railings to get down faster. I know people are coming for me, and I suddenly feel the gravity of what I have done. I am a terrorist. I have destroyed a city, killed thousands and perhaps millions of people. The whole country will be looking for me, and I am now a fugitive. How can I live with what I've done? With so much blood on my hands? I wake up.

...

I'm in a house that I don't remember, perhaps we're visiting someone, and in the downstairs bedroom closet there is a hidden panel that my brothers and I discover and slide off to remove a gaping hole leading into the house. We crawl inside, and realize that it's the opening of a cave that goes deep into the house. It's impenetrably dark, and there's a coolness in the air. We crawl through tight passages until reaching a narrow hole in the path that I'm too afraid to go through. A few people continue on through the tight opening, but I turn around and go back. Some time later, we return to the house and go to the bedroom closet expecting to find the cave. Instead, there is a man there, and there are empty rafters in what looks like an unfinished basement. He says that he is working on remodeling the place, and that the cave is no longer there.

...

A canyon appears down below me, with sandy sides and a sand trail that leads down to long wavy light-blue rocks that appear to form the bottom of the canyon. It looks like there is water in-between all of the wavy rock parts, and the parts can shift back and forth, revealing eternally deep drops between them as well. The sand on the edge of the canyon is unstable, and I fear falling into the steep drops filled with water. I see a man slip and fall down into one of these crevasses, an infinite abyss that narrows and where the man will slide to a halt and suffocate to death from the pressure on his lungs. I know that there is water there, and I know that you can't swim in it, and I know that when those two rock slats move back together the man will be crushed horridly between the rocks, and that he is drowning. I hear his screams as he falls deeper into the chasm, screams the water does not muffle.

Then I must walk on the wavy rock slats, slats that are long enough to span the whole canyon but barely wide enough for a foot to stand on, like a grand deck of wavy cards set on its side. Walking across them, I can feel them shifting under my weight, and I step carefully from one platform to the next over what could be my watery grave. The colors around me are rich reds and blues, and even the browns appear vibrant and concentrated in their hues. Large rock forms half cover the place where we are, and the sky is not bright. I wake up.

...

I am falling through the sky above a vast dark desert in the nighttime, skydiving with a few others. Deep purples and blues fill the sky, and the ground below is flat and dusty except for the occasional rocky mountain that juts its way out of the nothingness. When I fall far enough, I straighten my body and soar back up into the sky almost instantaneously, feeling no wind or noise around me at all. I fall again, the thrill of falling consuming me, then soar back up into the sky again, and again. When I've had my fill of the falling, I let myself continue to fall to the blackish-maroon earth. A parachute opens and I appear to be watching myself land underneath the chute from a third-person perspective that is already on the ground. Then I'm back in my body, my feet hitting the dirt hard. In the darkness, I see the others who have landed close to me, nameless figures who I know are my friends from some part of my life. There is a large metal warehouse-like building close to me and the others, something that feels like a secret we have been kept from, but also familiar. It takes a few minutes to walk to the building, then we enter through large metal doors and creep through the dark hallways, unsure of what secrets or security we will find. After wandering through the winding hallways for some amount of time, I wake up.

...

G O D   D E A T H   S T A R T

I'm in what appears to be a room in a high school, perhaps a chorus room where the floor has multiple levels so that seated students can see over each other to the teacher. There are many people, more than a dozen but less than thirty, many of them my friends, and all of us are sitting in red plastic metal-legged chairs.

Some of my friends are reading a book, a small paperback book that is completely absorbing their attention. The words "GOD DEATH START" appear on the front, and I ask someone sitting next to me what the book is. I learn that one of my friends is the author, and it's already sold millions of copies. I never touch the book or read anything inside of it, but for some reason I can sense the feeling of the book. It's as if the book's meaning is sending out vibrations, and they reach a natural frequency inside of me, resonating with something deeper than a casual glance.

I'm excited for my friend the author, yet also stirred with envy at their success. This envy sticks to my mind like plaque, causing me to question the intentions of the book I will write once I wake up.

Then I wake up.

...

The plains stretch out in front of me, forever it seems. The landscape is alive with beautiful colors, the colors of the desert amplified and darkened without the blinding sun above me. It's not dark outside, but it isn't bright either — I don't know where the sun is. My family was hiking with me, but they took a different route at some point to see a great canyon. I stayed up here on the plains, climbed a plateau, and now I look out over this great expanse of land. I know that I am alone, but I'm not lonely. There is a little emptiness inside of me, but the incredible vastness of the world before me fills another part of me, a part that you never realize is empty until the first time it is filled. I feel a kind of depth that is not joyful, it is not spiritual, it is something else. A feeling of independence and the knowledge that I am alive — those things are certainly part of it. I see large billowing clouds with dark outlines, flowing dusty golden and brown grasses filling the plains, and the broken rocks of the landscape that have been worn by time. But mostly, there are the feelings inside of me, and there are the colors. Then I wake up.

START

If you had been born fifty years from now, or fifty years before now, you would be completely different. I don't mean unrecognizable: you would probably look about the same. I mean that your personality would essentially be someone else's, and you wouldn't look through the same eyes that *you*-you look through right now. If you were to read this sentence, you wouldn't read it the same way. Everything about your perception would be changed by how you had grown up.

Much in the same way, personalities don't exist as separate from the entities to which they are attached. You cannot have a personality, you are a personality. The personality is you. You're not just some "you" floating out the in the void, picking up personality characteristics. Those characteristics are part of the definition of who "you" are. Likewise, your body parts help comprise that definition. And your environment. You can't exist without your environment. You can't just float in a complete void of nothing else — the things around you, inside of you, those help define you. This is why it is so important to turn our critical eye to the outside as well as the inside.

Think about every human on this planet as an experiment. We are all experiments, seven billion of us all roaming different parts of the earth with different friends and family doing different things with our lives. Different numbers of our social ties are abusive, or loving, alive or dead. We read different books, watch different movies, go to different schools. Each experiment is vastly complicated with innumerable variables influencing each grand and miniscule aspect of our lives.

Like all experiments, there are going to be a variety of different results because of all of these different inputs and conditions. Some people are going to hit the experimental jackpot, living lives of fame or fortune or great accomplishment. Many will die lonely and alone, known for nothing. Some will effortlessly have dazzling health, while others will struggle their whole lives just to feel ok. Occasionally, one will lead a revolution. A Gandhi, or MLK, or Jesus will lead a life that inspires millions to action. This kind of phenomenally improbable event is to be expected every now and then, much like the formation of life itself. Sometimes, perhaps equally likely as the Gandhi's of the world, terrible dictators exist, having grown up in just the right conditions for their tyranny to affect unfortunate masses of people. Those people affected are also experiments, and they were unfortunately in the wrong place at the wrong time.

The pessimist will take this knowledge as a condemnation of any hope they have at leading a fulfilling or meaningful life. The optimist will understand the unique position held by every living thing on this planet, and will use this knowledge to achieve a greater understanding of the variables contributing to his or her characteristics.

And somewhere else, someone stares out a window and knows that both the pessimist and the optimist will die someday, and that it is only their experience of life and their effect on the experiences of others that matters.

...

q

=

53113799281676709868958820655246862732 9593

11772703192319944413820040355986085 22

4273916250226522928566888932 94

86246501015346579337652 707

239409519978766587 351

9438312708353 93

2190317 28

127

PART III

Thomas turns from the window and paces slowly back to his chair, soaking in the strange feelings in the room. He lowers himself down to the soft cushion, straightens the crinkles in his pants, and leans over the chess table to reassess what is happening on the board. He moves a knight forward and to the middle. He leans back and looks at the man across from him. "You lot are pretty simple, you know?" God looks into Thomas's eyes and grins, like one might grin at a gerbil.

Thomas wasn't used to being called simple. There were several things he was used to being called, such as 'asshole', 'racist pig', even 'genius', but never 'simple'. In fact, the only people in the world he found he could call simple were Americans. Money, sex, shiny cars and big houses. Oh, and guns. They were a simple bunch.

"Simple. Well, that might be a new one for me. I think human beings can be trite, they can be angry and malicious and they can be jealous and petty, but they can also be good. They can be virtuous, kind, intelligent and creative. But I can't say I've ever thought of humans as simple," he says.

"Bah, then you haven't thought hard enough. Typical, of course. You just haven't seen something complex, Tom. Sorry old boy, you just haven't. None of you lot have." The man moves a white castle from the corner of the board toward his king in the middle. Thomas puts his elbow on the edge of the chair and leans his face on his hand so that his cheek smushes up toward his eyes, eyes that are staring at that unpalatable man, when suddenly the man moves forward quickly in his seat with a stern and concerned look on his face. "Ah ah ah, Thomas, no slouching or putting hard elbows on the chair arms. Soft rests only, please, gentle leans." Thomas hurriedly removes his elbow and sits up straight. "Thank you. Now let's not do that again."

Thomas clears his throat, awkwardly. What a way to die, he thought. Being stuck in the ground might be more peaceful than this. "Why, exactly, may I not place 'hard elbows' on the chair arms? Is that not what they are for?" This is the height of ridiculity.

"Of course not," the man replies, dumbfounded. "They are for resting your arms, resting, not leaning your whole body into the side of the chair. That's ridiculous. Now, it's your move again. I would appreciate you not holding up the game further by wandering about or being disruptive in general." What a way to die, indeed. Ironically, Heaven did bear many similarities to the Catholic school Thomas had once attended as a child. Perhaps they had gotten it right all along.

Thomas moves his knight further out, and God inches his queen forward, directly in front of a black pawn and the black knight that had been progressing out. Thomas shoots a bishop out from the back, all the way across the board next to a bishop and diagonal to a knight. God moves his bishop toward Thomas one space. Thomas smiles and moves his attention to the other side of the board, sliding his knight ahead further and into a space where it was attacking the queen and a knight. God moves the queen, Thomas takes the knight, only to lose his own knight the next turn to God's pawn.

"You're stuck on your earth still, Thomas, all of you are still stuck on that one planet. I don't count your little adventures in orbit, or whatever other small claims you've made on progress, your moon-hopping play-time. This whole universe that I created, and you've barely scratched the surface after billions of years. It frustrated me for the longest time, it saddened me. Disappointed. I'm just hoping the next evolution of your kind does a little better for itself. Maybe they won't wreck the place as badly."

Thomas huffs. "I've never met anymore more unpleasant than you," the words spurt out of Thomas's mouth, "whoever you are."

The middle-aged man rolls his eyes, mouth open and loudly sighing. "OH, you ungrateful simple soul. Listen to me, I'm God. God, you nincompoop. And, since you broached the topic of things you've never done, you never did lots of things, Thomas, did you…?" He pauses for a moment, and Thomas waits in uncomfortable anticipation of what was coming next. "Actually… I usually don't do this, but I looked into your life a bit, to play the part while we had our quirky little game of chess, since you people usually think I know everything about you. But it was depressing, frankly, so I didn't look too deeply because of how depressed I usually get thinking about your species. Pretty sad, huh? Your existence? You weren't the most cordial, so fixated on your little chess bubble that you couldn't get out to meet and mingle with the rest of the primates. You were hateful, full of loathing, and fond of making enemies with those you knew nothing about. Yes, I read some of the things you said, in public even. Not a nice person, Tom. Not very nice." The man has a sad look in his eyes now, looking at Thomas with a slight frown, his voice low and smoky, sorrowful. His words are slow and deliberate. "I'm sorry that your life is over, frankly, because now you can't fix any of it, you know. I pity you. All spent on…on this," he says, waving his pale hand over the chess set. Icy blue blood shows through translucent veins, like viewing the ocean through dirty glass. "Why would you waste your conscious hours on this?"

Thomas sits lifeless for a moment, peering downward at his own hands and the blood through his own veins, blood still impossibly flowing through his veins, then his eyes moisten over the slightest bit and a heaviness fills the front of his face. He blinks, wipes at the tears quickly, and sniffs. He moves his other knight forward to take God's pawn.

GOD

The only reason that some people heard a clock chime was because the clock was running a little early. The rest of humanity never heard the first "ding", because at the precise moment the hour changed all humans were obliterated from the earth. It wasn't a painful obliteration, or a tortuous annihilation, it was very peaceful in fact. Well, as peaceful as death is I suppose.

Unpiloted planes crashed, many forks full of food were dropped onto chairs and floors, and in general there were many thumps and thuds and whirrs and plops as various human-held or human-worn things cascaded to the floor. The dogs who had been on a walk with their guardians were suddenly freed once and for all into the world (finally, they thought), and the animals ran and played and fought and barked, all without human intervention. Cars freely continued in their trajectories until their collisions with various objects, sitting there in a sad entanglement where engines sometimes continued clunking along until the gas ran out.

Not a single person remained to say "Aha! I told you so!" No one was left to speculate about the end of the world, or to hypothesize, or to run news broadcasts on the disappearances. No one wondered about the disappearances, and no one said the word "apocalypse", because there was simply no one left to wonder or say anything.

Meanwhile, somewhere outside of the fabric of spacetime as humans knew it, God sadly considered the earth and all of the people who had just disappeared. They had so much potential, he thought to himself. Their spirits were ripe with curiosity, their hearts often blooming like fruit trees in the spring. The golden glow of goodness sometimes rang within their hearts, and God delighted in the sound. But, he thought, in the end there was nothing that could be done.

Thousands of years he gave them to behave as suitably moral creatures. He believed they could do it, he truly did, but their progress was simply too give-and-take. One step forward, two back, five forward, four back. A net sum of zero, and oh the suffering that had been endured because of it! Because of that one unhappy and unfulfilling Zero! Zero progress, despite the technology, despite the medicine, nothing was moved forward one fraction of a bit in the ways that mattered. He often looked on in horror, cringing as millions of people, billions of them in fact, made the same mistakes over and over again, despite thousands and thousands of generations before them who did the same, mistakes that brought suffering and terror upon themselves and other creatures. He desperately wanted to believe that their love could outpower the hate, but in the end it was too much to bear. I am a God of love, he thought. This was truly the most loving thing he could have done, he knew. But it still saddened him.

Perhaps he would try again in the future, perhaps with an animal whose capacity for love greatly outgrew their capacity for intelligence. They would suffer and die still, as life commanded, but with greater dignity and more fulfilled lives. They would know it was all worth it, and there would be no evils at the hands of each other. Perhaps he would instill in them a skepticism for authority, an inherent sense of justice and compassion. He would have to figure out a way to get rid of jealousy — perhaps asexual creatures would fare better. It would be best if they shunned power and acclaim, too, to avoid saviors and dictators, instead sharing a common focus of always working together in joint effort. Either way, nothing more for now, he thought. For now he was content to wander the galaxy alone, breathing beauty into the far reaches of the universe, letting the other beings of planet earth live out the rest of their time without the influence of their crueler sisters and brothers.

DEATH

Your body is a ship, and every cell is a plank of wood. Every single day of your life, somewhere on the order of 60 billion cells die. This isn't a traumatic death for them, this is a pre-programmed death called apoptosis. These cells can be skin cells, blood cells, or any other cells in the body, all which die and get replaced many times throughout your life.

Except for brain cells, interestingly, which more or less last your whole lifetime and are not replaced when they die. More on that in a minute.

So then, hypothetically let's say that all of your cells that *can* be replaced are, some getting replaced every day, so that at some point after your birth all of your cells are now totally different cells from the ones you were born with. (Brain excluded.) Are you still the same person?

If every plank of wood on a ship is replaced, is it still the same ship?

Perhaps we say yes, it is the same ship. Perhaps we say yes, we are the same person. Wherein, then, lies the essence of the ship? The essence of us? It would seem that it couldn't lie in any one cell or cluster of cells, because all of those cells eventually get replaced. But maybe, we think, there is more to us than simply the cells we are composed up. There is also the unique *structure* of those cells and their relationships with each other. The blueprint of our bodies, in a sense. Maybe our true essence lies in the blueprint, and not in the specific cells that go into the final construction.

For us, at first glance there is a little bit of an easier way to find an answer to this problem. If our brain cells stay the same, and our brains are where the important parts of conscious "us" live, then our essence must lie somewhere in the cells and structuring of the brain.

Are the specific brain cells necessary, though, for us to still be us? If we were to switch them out one by one with identical but different cells, would we still be there on the other side looking through our own eyes? Or would it be someone different? And at what point would it become someone different?

If another person is created having exactly the same cells in exactly the same structure as you, is that person you? Whose eyes do you look out of? Your old ones? Or the new ones? Or both?

This question, incidentally, poses an interesting problem for teleportation. Teleportation, I presume, involves the dissolution of your atoms and the reassembling of them (or identical but different atoms) back into "you" in a different place. Since information can travel at the speed of light, but we obviously can't, this could potentially involve a very sophisticated 3D printer that simply receives a digital blueprint of your body from somewhere far away and then reconstructs you on the spot. In this way, interplanetary and interstellar travel would become much more feasible.

But after you get dissolved, turned into a blueprint, and reconstructed on the other side by our sophisticated body printer, this becomes exactly the problem discussed above — which "you" is the one that gets printed? Does your consciousness continue in the new place, or are you plunged into eternal darkness of nonexistence while another consciousness is created in your new body?

To complicate things, there's really no way to tell from the outside which "you" shows up. Philosophically, there may never be a way to tell. Because from the outside, everything would look exactly the same. This new person would look like you, sound like you, they would even *think* they were you. But none of that matters to you if *you* suddenly cease to exist, from *your* current perspective.

But then again, your nonexistence wouldn't matter to you either after you ceased to exist. Which makes the question even more difficult. Either way, I don't think I'll be teleporting anywhere anytime soon. (For philosophical reasons, of course.)

So where is the seat of your consciousness? This question has been bantered around for thousands of years, and it probably won't stop being an interesting and important question anytime soon. However, maybe we're now on the brink of figuring out enough about the brain to be able to say some meaningful things about consciousness from an experimental point of view. Maybe there is no single "center" for your consciousness. Maybe what you perceive as "I" is actually the complex cocktail of all of your senses and inputs being swirled around in your brain, with nothing to call the "center" of it all. Maybe there is. Maybe in some ways, our present consciousness is the end of a chain of slightly different consciousnesses that all no longer exist.

Here are some letters to consciousnesses that no longer exist.

...

Dear Steven,

If you're reading this, then something really weird and potentially impossible has happened.

Well actually, if you're reading this then you're most likely a future version of me who is reading this for a trip down memory lane or perhaps picked this up by mistake or something. But this isn't to you. This is to past me. Me from many years ago.

Which, if future me is reading this, is also your "past me" as well, I guess. Technicalities.

So, hello past me. You were pretty weird growing up. You still are weird — I mean, I'm still weird — but you were pretty freaking strange. Not in a bad way, just in a "most kids your age weren't pretending their pencils were rocket ships and riding them around the desk with their fingers in the seventh grade" way. But you also managed to start writing a book, the one about the end of the world via molten rocks exploding from the earth, and get that one dude interested in it. The big, lumbering guy in your class. So that's cool. You're a cool kid. Just strange. I dig it, now, as an older you.

You may not realize it yet actually, but you can trace your personality traits to a number of different factors that are all out of your control. Your genetics, your home life as a child, the cities you grew up in, the friends you made through the years, the kinds of books that were available to you. This isn't necessarily a bad thing. We're all experiments in life, you know, you and me included.

In case you're wondering, I'm still alive so you obviously haven't fucked up too badly. I have a pretty decent command of the English language, I graduated from college, I have a job. All of these things are considered mile markers of living a quasi-successful life, typically. So don't worry about any of that. But you should know that this doesn't mean you're going to have any easy life. Far from it. There are some hard times ahead of you kid, and some things are going to happen that will rock your world. Maybe I haven't even had the worst of it yet. Maybe another future me is writing another letter to me, telling me about all of the future horrible things that are going to happen. Or worse, maybe they're not able to write about it at all.

Ok, maybe this is a bit much for you. You're young, and I'm sorry if this freaks you out at all.

I want you to know that things are going to get hard, and sometimes you're going to feel like giving it all up, giving up on life, like you're so alone and things are never going to get better. I have news from the future: everyone feels this way at some point in their life, and it gets better. I promise you, it gets better. Don't give up, kid.

If I could force one idea into your brain it would be that other people matter. And even people who aren't people. Like, animals. You're going to realize one day that you are one life among many other lives, and that all of these lives can be happy and feel pain and do so many of the things you can do. And all these people around you, everyone around the world, have so many of the same dreams and aspirations and hopes as you.

People matter so much. It's weird to write that, and I bet it sounds kind of fru-fru and emotional and sappy or whatnot to you, but really take a moment to listen to what I'm saying and know that this is one of the deepest truths I've learned so far in my time on this planet. Everyone else is living their lives through their eyes like you are living your life through yours. Their experiences matter to you. Your experiences matter to them. They are the best things in your life. Remember that.

If I had time for a few more thoughts, I would let you know that lots of other things matter too. The unrelenting honest quest for truth should be the foundation for how you approach everything. An appreciation for beauty, wonder, and mystery will be your spirituality, as well as a love of how big and small everything can be. Many other wonderful and splendid things. Life is unimaginably beautiful and complex, and you should really dig in deep. Get your hands dirty. Figure things out.

But the art and science of living in this world with other living things is the most complex and important part of your life. Because it defines everything important about your life, whether you know it or not.

That's pretty much it for now, considering you will most likely never read this. Don't eat as much mac 'n' cheese as you have been. Oh, and the future really is full is all kinds of mind-blowing technology, but after a while you still wind up getting annoyed at how slow things are. Some things never change. Silly humans.

Good luck. Live and help live, you magnificent existence.

Future You

...

Dear Zach,

I haven't written you in a long time, and it feels weird not to talk. All those times in life that I have some crazy idea or I just want to hang out, you pop into my mind.

I've been listening to our music a lot recently, thinking about the good ol' days of While We're Up. It was awesome man, being on that crazy band adventure with you. That's the stuff life is made of, you know? So many memories. So many good times.

Remember when we decorated the dining hall for our album release? It was Valentine's Day, so we bought pink and white balloons and streamers and put them absolutely everywhere. We stayed up all night doing it in secret, wondering what the dining hall workers would think when they showed up the next morning. We pumped pop-punk tunes from a phone and sank along with the reverberations of the echoing stone walls and floor.

Or the night that it rained so much it practically flooded the campus. It was cold, but that didn't stop us from putting on swim suits and running barefoot through every puddle. I'll never forget sprinting across the vast athletic fields that were covered with over a foot of water, motionless water that reflected all of the starlight and building lights back up at us, a perfect glistening void in the middle of that building-filled university. That space felt infinite, like we were running through the stars.

I often wonder where we'd be now, if you were still here. Would we still be in the band together? Would we maybe be doing music separately? Would I still have gotten such a heart for animals, or a passion for the power of technology? I think a lot about you and the amazing things you would've done in your life. Life was just getting going for us, you know? Finally out of school. Finally free to really just pour ourselves into something. And it was working! I mean, we were pretty hot stuff. The tour was going well, people liked us. As a duo, I think we might have been unstoppable.

Anyway, I'm going for a bike ride now. I don't longboard now like I did when we were in school, but I want to start again. I know I won't ever find anyone to replace you, but it would be nice to have a friend to go boarding with. Sometimes I wish I could relive those days. But I know, only in my memory. Just know I miss you. I wish you were here to bike with me.

Steven

START

The visions for possible futures and presents and pasts are endless. We create them in our minds, our bodies, and then in our worlds. Let them continue.

...

Unfortunately, in this world society is positively wasteful in their resources. It's a natural consequence of innovators being so far removed from the majority of the population, but nevertheless it's a tragedy.

Consider this example. It can be shown rather simply that there is one primary budgeting and finance tracking system that works well for the majority of human beings. This system has a name, let's call it Money, and people would be better off if they were to log all of their expenses with this system. Not only that, those who developed Money put great effort into making sure that it is as automated and simple as possible, so that there is very little upkeep. Simply connect the system to your banks, and it does all the work for you.

Yet, only a few million people currently use the system. What of the other millions? The other billions? If they keep track of their finances at all, it's with a less-efficient and effective system. These lesser systems not only take longer to set up, but they also take longer to actually use, which means more wasted time up-front as well as more continually wasted time. Daily, weekly wasted time and energy. Many of these people may even try to create their own system of watching their money, complicated and archaic systems using spreadsheets and paper and things. This energy being spent by them is, in effect, redundant. If more than one person is working on the same system, that energy is wasted. Here, millions and millions of people are all working on broken systems.

Now, take the sum total of all of those wasted hours, all of that wasted energy. It adds up to an exorbitant amount of time! All that time, spent doing something completely unnecessary, something that has been perfected elsewhere by people who made it their mission to perfect it.

Consider also, that this is just one example of waste in this world. This example can easily be extrapolated to any and nearly all systems. There's a good system out there — most people don't use it. The extra effort those people spend by not using the good system is time and energy wasted. Time that isn't being spent on getting healthier, or having conversations with friends, or reading, or bettering oneself.

...

In this world, all of that extra energy is actually saved and used in non-redundant ways. The energy and natural resources crisis is long over because the majority of human effort was spent on innovation until workable solutions were found, ensuring healthy futures for the people currently living and their future generations. Solar energy's efficiency ratio was maximized, nuclear energy was safely implemented around the globe, and massive campaigns compelled businesses and people to produce and buy products at healthy, sustainable levels. Many terrible diseases, as well as genetic and neurological disorders were then cured in a short amount of time due to the countless minds working together and innovating across hundreds of thousands of ideas.

There are still large problems to be solved in this world, but one by one workable solutions are getting figured out because of the concentrated efforts of humanity. This world truly shows the power of cooperation in creating massive change for the better, and people are incredibly thankful that things didn't turn out any other way.

Every action we choose to make is not only a choice for that action,

but also a choice against all other actions.

PART IV

Thomas's heart was slowly filling with cold water. He had to say something. "Where were you then, my whole life? Who are you, some god who just creates things and then lets them be? Doesn't interact with his creations? Why would you do that? My whole goddamn life, I fought against you. I fought belief, I thought it was poison. I ridiculed those who believed in you. I wanted to believe, I just needed a sign. Some proof, some evidence, some interaction. Where were you?" Thomas's voice is shaking now, and his eyes are wide and hurt.

God moves his bishop up to take Thomas's pawn, pinning both his queen and his rook against the back row. A moment passes in silence. Thomas notices a small hint of smoke in the air, like a candle was put out half an hour ago in a room down the hall. "You know," the man starts, "I've only listened to human music a couple of times. I occasionally drop by and see the latest artistic creations or scientific developments or things like that," God says, pulling his well-ironed shirt sleeves slightly down his arms and out of his suit coat sleeves a bit more. "That piece over there, actually," he lifts his arm slowly and points a lazy finger over the top of his shoulder at *Le Bassin Aux Nymphéas* hanging on a wall over a small table where a few old books sat, "is one of Monet's. I did have a small soft spot for Monet... He was a rare one who came the closest, I think. But mostly, I just don't know why. I don't know why people consider these things to be noteworthy. Not to be rude, you understand... please don't take offense." God stares down at the chess board and clears his throat. "There are just better things to do."

Thomas stares, mouth open, dumbstruck.

"I always hate telling people that. It never goes well. By the way," God says, "that table over there is for you. Food, for if you get hungry." He flicks his hand in a circular motion over in the direction of the window leading out into the abyss, and Thomas notices what he'd apparently missed while gazing out of the glass: there was a very new-looking wooden table that he doubted had ever been used before, like a dinner table but with only one chair, and on it were several plates of food. Some fruit, some bread, a bottle of wine. He looks back at the chess game, then slowly moves his queen away from the attacking bishop.

"Lots of people search for me Tom, that's what I've heard from others as well. You know, I want to say that I understand the yearning to be engaged with me, but I'm not sure I do when you have access to all of humankind who share your interests. It does wear on me, too, hearing again and again that you all are depending on me. I don't see why you lot want to rely on me so much. Have a little pluck. That's what I do.

"I lament not being able to explain to you how my time is filled, or the intricacies of my work and its importance; truly, it grieves me, but I can't! I just can't. You wouldn't understand, couldn't, there's no possible way for your to comprehend. The most advanced transformations of the most inconceivable forms. At one time, I held onto hope that mathematicians would eventually approach my realm of inquiry. I hold that hope no longer. That's my world, Tom. You have yours, I have mine. I simply don't have time for your every want and wish. Let me be so bold to say it's a little selfish of you, I think, to desire that of me. A little selfish of humans. Frankly." He moves his other bishop out and to the center of the board, attacking the same area as the first.

A cold silence passes between the two. Thomas moves his knight in to take a pawn, the man moves his bishop back out from Thomas's side of the board, now attacking the black queen. Black castle out one space, out from behind the row of pawns. Check. God moves his king one inside to avoid it. Queen is still open for the taking unless Thomas moves it. God coughs quietly, then checks his watch, another faceless gold-plated circle full of throbbing lines of light and shape. Thomas moves… his bishop, back two spaces to attack another bishop, queen still unprotected. God smiles and sighs in finality as he makes the game-changing move. He moves his bishop onto the space where Thomas's queen is, slowly removing the queen from the board.

"Not really sure what you were thinking there, Tom. Do you think you're playing well, or have you stumbled in error? I just want to know how I'm doing, of course, as this is my inaugural game."

Thomas remains quiet, and takes God's other bishop with his. Check. God moves his king further into the corner, surrounded by the back of the board on one side, his castle on another, and a solid row of pawns out front. Thomas moves a knight up, second row from the back, beside the row of pawns. Check again. God frowns, moving his king back to the space where it just was, with Thomas's knight now blocking the bishop that used to be attacking him there. Thomas moves his knight back out to take a pawn, now the bishop is attacking the man's king again. Check. God shuffles in his seat uncomfortably, leaning forward slightly to look at the board. His way out is blocked by Thomas's castle on the far end of the board; his only option is to move the king back in or futilely block the bishop's attack with a piece that would then only get taken. He moves his king back into the corner. Thomas moves his knight back to the same space, putting the now-angry man back into check.

"Now you're just being annoying, and petty, you squabbling fool. Don't be upset that I speak the truth of you and your kind."

Thomas simply says "your turn", and nothing more.

God moves his king back away from the corner yet again, only for Thomas to move his knight again, this time in a different direction, so that the bishop is now attacking the king still.

"I simply don't understand, why do people get so offended at the truth of the matter. You've been created, you're simple, now I do other things. Perhaps I'm not terribly interested in your art, your music, your personal affairs. They're yours to deal with, not mine. If you want the truth, there it is. Embrace it, Tom." He moves his king back into the corner, and then on the other side of the board Thomas takes a bishop with a pawn, the same bishop that had taken his queen. The middle-aged man breathes, then moves his queen toward the offending bishop and away from the now impending attack of Thomas's other castle, recently freed by the moved pawn. "I even created this place for you, I created a Heaven so that you humans could have one since you wanted it so badly. Wasn't that nice of me?" Thomas moves the castle all the way up to the middle of the board, coming to rest beside the man's queen. The rally subsides, and Thomas smiles a weary smile.

<u>GOD</u>

Perhaps let's not ask who or what god is, let's ask how we define god.

Suppose we define god as that other "you" inside of you, the one that provides ideas and thoughts out of nowhere, the one that sometimes steers you to make better choices. Something like a conscience, something like creativity, something like love. This god can be transcendent and mysterious and inspiring, in part because of the vast complexities that go into it. Morality, consciousness, and creativity are all things that still elude exacting scientific description. For now, they could serve to embody the definition of a helpful and elusive god in us all, yet still colloquially distinct from us as well.

Or let's define god to be the whole universe and everything in it. Every last piece of everything that exists and the space holding it all together. Is this god conscious? Certainly a large number of the pieces of god are conscious, like you or I. But as an analogy, if all of the cells in my body had their own minute consciousness, would that add to my perception of the world at all? I don't think so, unless those individual pieces were connected to my larger consciousness in a way that could convey information and knowing.

But, still, consciousness is a centralized entity that perceives itself and the world around. We fit both of those criteria. Most humans do, except for those with severe brain damage. Most animals do. And we are, in some sense, connected with the rest of the universe, are we not? Even if only in a smattering of subatomic particles over the whole course of the universe; a proton in my brain that was maybe in that star, before floating across stretches of space to land on that planet, to get ingested by that creature, to touch that neutron. Perhaps we are the consciousness of god. Maybe god has trillions of distinct consciousnesses. Maybe our consciousness isn't as consolidated as we think it is. Maybe in some very real way, I am you and you are me.

Or we could define god to be the foundations of logic and mathematics, those things that remain true whether or not we discover them. But then again, is there anything that remains true if we do not define it as such, or is definition the very heart of truth? Does $1 = 1$ if there is no one there to define it as such? These statements may become meaningless without entities to perceive them, but maybe god becomes meaningless as well without those entities. If we define god to be logic, mathematics and those unerring foundations of reality that we live in, then god is also inextricably wound into the fabric of *our* existence, since logical axioms presuppose a consciousness. This is exactly what god *should* be, though, to many people — if god does not contain the impression of humanity somewhere within it, however minimally, then our time is best spent conceiving of other gods.

God might be defined to be the unknowable: those things that we simply cannot know, because of whatever physical or logical limitations may exist. Yet what better place to position a deity than just outside of the realm of things we can learn and understand? The story of humanity is driven by the quest to know the unknowable, to understand the inconceivable, and to use the knowledge we learn to position ourselves higher in the ordering of the universe. The unknowable provides space for exactly the kaleidoscopic spirituality that we yearn to spill through the shining veins of our confusing lives. The unknowable is worthy of our worshipful devotion.

Or we might define god as the negative space to the unknowable, or a subset of that space: the known. God, then, is greater than any one of us, for who among us can claim to know all that is known? Should the world be scraped bare at this moment, our combined knowledge would be required to begin rebuilding civilization as we know it. No one of us has the full requisite knowledge to reconstruct anything worthy of being built. It requires all of us.

If we define god as the things that we know, collectively, then the quest for understanding becomes a quest for the divine. The greater our knowledge of the universe, the greater our knowledge of god. This sense of learning and knowing as something transcendent should mesh very well with the inclinations of the bookish, the academic, the dedicated, the devoted. This god is not for the disinterested or the lazy, and the hard work involved should appeal to those in modern and classical monastic traditions. Dedication and perseverance in the face of adversity are traits common to the sciences and religious devotion alike. Those who pass the trials of seminary are likely to experience similar tribulations as those in medical school.

Regardless of how we choose to define god, it is imperative to realize that the conceptualization of god is always a definition, even if that definition is too implicit to be understood is specific terminology. More importantly is the understanding that our definitions of god rarely match each other's, even if we happen to be in the same religion or tradition.

Most importantly, every concept is a definition. What are yours?

DEATH

Let's say there existed a man.

Let's say Zach was his name, Zach Booher. Let's say he was a best friend and beloved musician, a bandmate, a man of extraordinary talent and spirit who had been a shining presence in the room all his life, a force to be reckoned with. Let's say he was a man who died, like all other men must do at some point. Like all women must do. All living things. Let's say he died in a car crash, as many people do these days, a car crash that my brother and I lived through, a car crash that involved no other cars and no fault of any conscious being, but merely one unfortunate permutation of atoms in the universe. One unfortunate permutation.

One unfortunate permutation of atoms is all it takes to wreak complete havoc on the lives of us human beings, but we never see these things as just permutations of matter. We see things like causality, and we see that there are intentions, and we believe in things like destiny and fate. Our own wills and thoughts and dreams become entangled with the happenings of the universe, and so we never see these things as the mere arrangement of pieces of the universe. Some arrangements are those that we enjoy, that are favorable to our lives. Some arrangements are those that kill us. But mere unbiased arrangements is all they are, inherently.

Let's say that car crash, the one that matters to me, that one accident out of the tens of thousands of other ones that probably happened on that same exact day in 2012, those tens of thousands of accidents that ended the lives of dozens of other people on average, let's consider that this one specific car crash is the event where I could most accurately taste the flavors of death, where the cold slumber nearly had me wrapped in its arms. Let's say, in fact, that I may as well have died in that instant. Or rather, reworded, that I wouldn't know I had died, if I had.

All I know is that I didn't die, because I didn't. Which, in itself, is a very strange thought to have.

There's a blackness of unawareness that exists during vast stretches of sleep when you are completely unconscious. In those hours, anyone could die and not know it. The blackness you can imagine (or not imagine) is what I experienced (or, more truthfully, did not experience until after the experience was over), but this blackness was not in the context of sleep, sleep which brings a greater lucidity to the event. Or something analogous to lucidity. Something divergent from dying.

When a solid and heavy sharp mass of something makes contact with your head as your car is executing barrel rolls down searing black pavement of a two-lane highway in Wisconsin and *then* your consciousness turns into black nothingness...well, that's as close to dying as you can expect to get before the real thing, I suppose. That's something quite unlike sleep, in many ways that are important.

And perhaps in this first, preliminary death, perhaps there are CDs scattered across the road that won't be there in your final death. There is a greater sense of urgency in this near-death, maybe. All of the greens are even greener than you imagined. And the people all have accents.

But we all have accents, don't we? We just happen to be unaware of one of those accents for much of our lives.

There is a saying about a peace that surpasses all understanding, a concept that seems to resonate with many people but that has never found its natural frequency inside of me. I have not discovered a peace greater than the one imparted by understanding — at least, not a true peace. Not a meaningful peace, one that exists without the aid of some brain-altering hormones or other chemicals. Understanding has brought me a greater peace than I could ever imagine, peace that surpasses even my own hard-wired biases and anxieties. Peace that surpasses my spirituality.

Understanding, in this specific instance of my life that we are currently discussing, is an understanding of the biological and neurological events that were happening in the moments of the crash. By understanding the composition of the brain, as well as my own experiences, one can be reassured that Zach did not experience pain at his death, or if he did then it wasn't much and it wasn't for long. Our minds and bodies are beautiful instruments that can be kind to us even when they are bruised and damaged, even moments from their end.

My own personal near-death experience was chaotic, jarring, and maybe a bit painful, but not excruciatingly so. The most unpleasant bit of it was after the fact when there was time to recreate the scene over and over again. The experience itself was too fast to really know what was happening, too fast to consciously experience agony or any other higher-order mental processes. Just a brief blip of noise in your consciousness, then black. The only difference between me and Zach was that I eventually experienced things again, that "sum of experiences" thing we call consciousness. I had more experiences, while his experiences ended at that one moment. At least, that's what I have the most reason to believe.

Which is a fucking shame, if there ever was one.

It's kin to the fallacious Great Beethoven argument, which goes like this. Suppose you have a syphilitic father, a mother with tuberculosis, and they already have four children between them: one is blind, one died, one is deaf and dumb, and one has tuberculosis. The mother is pregnant again – would you terminate the pregnancy? If you say yes, as many might, then the arguer goes "You evil thing! You would have murdered Beethoven." The argument is supposed to show how all lives have meaning, and therefore aborting even one child is to potentially keep the world from knowing the next great so-and-so. Or something like that.

This argument, incidentally, is also very wrong.

First of all, the premises don't hold – Beethoven was the *oldest* surviving child (the first died), and neither his mother nor his father had syphilis or tuberculosis at the time of his birth – but perhaps we can forgive them this. The argument stretches some things, but surely in the history of humanity there had to be some youngest child born to a terribly afflicted family who turned out to be one of the greats. The point of the argument is not necessarily to be factually correct, it is to show you how you don't know the potential worth of any human fetus that is on its way to being born. But perhaps, instead of aborting Beethoven, we were to abort Hitler instead. Would you still disapprove of this decision? Surely we can't base the argument off of human worth anymore, because nearly everyone would agree that it would have been better if Hitler hadn't existed. So we can show pretty simply one of the flaws in the argument. There are many other.

The beginning of a life, human or other, is a very complicated issue and the facts involved are much deeper and more tangible than the very-unknowable "future worth of this specific human", a measurement which doesn't hold up to strong analysis, especially considering that depending on the stage of pregnancy, you are very literally regarding a clump of cells that has zero sentience. Even once the formation of a body and all the necessary systems starts, there are studies that suggest sentience may not be present in the fetus until halfway through the pregnancy, at the very very earliest. It may not occur until much closer to birth.

In our story, though, whatever mechanisms were at play in the universe caused a very real and very sudden elimination and abortion of the consciousness known as Zach Booher, a man who was a fully sentient and developed individual. We all already knew that he was a creative powerhouse: he had created and was creating and would have created in the future. Everyone knew that. Time, resources, and love had all been poured into this being for years upon years. He had made it through the tumultuous period of childhood into the independence of adulthood, and was poised to accomplish wonderful things in his lifetime.

Everyone can have great ideas, but Zach actually followed through — and that second part is what really counts, a life lesson I learned much later in life than I would have liked to. Remember this, all you people (myself still included) who want to simply birth ideas and then let others do the heavy lifting. Everyone has amazing ideas. The only thing that counts is if you have the motivation to make them happen.

So it wasn't like we were unsure if some potentially soon-to-be-aborted fetus was going to accomplish great things. This man, this brother of mine, Zach, he was already doing that. He was on course for a lifetime of really badass stuff. His creations were still rough around the edges, of course, but he was already great and working so freaking hard to get better. If you ever stop and wonder about all of the greats who might've been, Zach is among them. His name very well could have been written in books that people in the future actually care to read. Perhaps it still will be. There's much in life that is not known.

So that's one of the real tragedies in my existence and the existence of Zach's friends and family, that we never get to see how his life would have played out. Another tragedy is that he didn't get to live it. His blip of consciousness was cut short. Which is endlessly tragic, truly, the death of a creative soul before its time. The universe did a terrible wrong to end that life.

But that's only to be expected in life, you know? Sometimes bad people live on to do terrible things, sometimes good people die before doing more wonderful things. Which leads to my next major point.

The large-scale universe, simply put, just doesn't care. It has no caring apparatus, no inferior parietal cortex full of empathy. This point has been argued about over and over again by philosophers throughout time, a point which might even serve as evidence for one side of the argument if viewed in the right light. In fact, *every experience* of *everything ever* is evidence for one side of the argument or the other, and in my view the worldview that holds the most weight under this historical scrutiny is one where our place is no more special than we make it. This lovely universe of ours a whirling smoothie of particles and energy (or as I learned from a Sean Carroll lecture, fields and their particles), and the fact that we're here in the mix is for no super-universal reason and makes no difference to anything except other living things. The only reason anything is important or has purpose is because we living things desire those qualities and because we attribute them to things. Without consciousness, it's just rocks and stuff. Rocks and stuff by themselves have no interests. No cares. No loves.

However, the correct combinations of rocks and stuff do have cares, and loves, and interests. We are one of those combinations of rocks and stuff. This is one of the craziest things about existence.

Nothing is working in our favor except for ourselves and other people. This isn't some fatalistic doomsday message; it's a message of inspiration. If you want something awesome to happen, you need to get out there and create it. Animal sacrifices to Yahweh didn't make the iPhone, and the angel Gabriel didn't invent solar or penicillin. These things all came from the extremely hard work of your fellow human beings. As did modern medicine. As did warfare. As did refugees. As did guns and knives. As did bandages.

Here we are, responsible for the things that we've been inclined to contribute to super-universal "Others". Aren't we powerful.

Death may be the number one motivator of us all, because death is also in some sense why we're all here. The brutal churning forces of gravity and molecules, the relentless involuntary push of evolution, eliminating everything except what happens to survive. Death birthed us.

Or rather, we are the negative space created by the portrait of death.

This fact is so crucial that I want to state it again, because once you understand it the entire world will make infinitely more sense in very real, very concrete ways.

We are the current ending of a long chain of things that survived and reproduced. The sole determining factor in us existing right now wasn't truth, love, intelligence, or anything else. The sole determining factors were survival and reproduction. If you look at society, this should make perfect sense. Other things may come along for the ride, but survival determines life. This is the deepest of trivialities.

And so we survive, wishing to live because the desire to live helps us survive. Cyclical, unintuitive, but true nonetheless. We are burdened with questions of "Why" for some reason, and there is no answer to "Why" in the sense that we classically want there to be an answer to "Why", but yet the truth provides a warm embrace once you forget the fear of how she looks. Every cold and unfeeling and brutal thing inexplicable by a theory of gentle guiding hands of existence, more explained by our present, infinite, mechanical, biological, breathing, living and dead universe. Perhaps our little sphere of blue and green will be the only positively spiked blip on the map of consciousness. Perhaps we are in a frothy sea of peaks, unawares. Yet alone, as a planet, our consciousness approaches singularity. It lies so far outside our comprehension we may never reach it. That's ok. I promise you, it's alright.

It's alright to be scared of death, just like it's alright to be afraid of clowns. That doesn't mean that fear is good. What makes sense is not necessarily good. Rape and torture make sense, yet they're some of the most horrific things that can be thought of. The senseless and brutal slaughter of animals for food makes sense, the treatment of animals like machines incapable of feelings makes sense. It's how our society runs, abusing other lifeforms for our benefit. Slavery, discrimination, child labor, sex trafficking. But these things are not good. Far from it, these are the stumbling blocks currently in our path to a better future. We must surpass them.

There are several major points in my life when I have been shown amazing love and compassion by 100% complete strangers. As I lay in the grass on the side of the highway, my bleeding head heavy with shock and my body feeling fairly numb and disconnected from itself, a lady knelt beside me and talked to me as someone else called an ambulance. The sun was hot on my face, unbelievably hot for Wisconsin I thought, even though I had never been to Wisconsin before, and the lady stood in the way of the sun so I could have shade. The nurses at the hospital were crazy nice, and I still remember the face of one male nurse in particular who helped me a lot. I remember when I came back a few days later and he had gotten a haircut so that I almost didn't recognize him. I remember my family, and my friends, and their love and support. I remember how Subway was one of the last meals my brother and I shared with Zach, and how we ate our sandwiches in a silence shared between sun-drained dreamers.

I console myself occasionally with the thought that all great women and men before us have endured the same ending, death and the obliteration of consciousness. Einstein, Emily Dickinson, the Buddha, Jesus, da Vinci. All dead. It brings me comfort, not in a bragging or powerful sense, but just knowing that others have gone before me. All others who have ever lived, and all those who will one day live, will die. This is reassuring. We all meet the same end.

The difference, of course, lies in how it ends.

And how we get there.

START

People rewire the vision center of their brains to feed directly into their devices. This leads to a massive side-effect where they can no longer use their eyes as well, but it's a trade-off most people are willing to make. After all, over 50% of their time spent awake is on some kind of device anyway (closer to 90% for the average person), so it's much more beneficial to them to have that digital information hardwired into their minds rather than use their poor and failing eyes to continually try to read screens.

As with all other technological advancements throughout time, there are some people who are resistant to the change, those who cry signs of the apocalypse. But slowly, as time passes, even these people find a way to adapt to the changes, and soon they are getting their vision hardwired to technology as well. This kind of technology never would have been possible before the days of self-driving cars and automated home food delivery, but those kinds of set-backs are now nonexistent. What's more, productivity has skyrocketed. People no longer get as tired working at their computers, which means they are able to be more efficient for longer periods of time. Contrary to the claims of those resistant to the change, the happiness and satisfaction of the average citizen remains the same.

Mostly.

...

P A R T   I V

code

=

199375939841848977777558351796430512226067

18521342126526665852664411 6419124

677907713975761396869779621 1635

3870275851713629289972 28

89391852131785564

5557454197053

3290188

836

880

8547034

7835666422868

28403645108195730

83560586415440795245 5834

2715204807124633771555550582655

7768221253577849820419326435 80782

53440148019624092827054118178518 1588099543

Outside of perception, things are not.

PART V

If I'm stuck here for a while anyway, Thomas thinks, I might as well get some damn answers. He ponders for a moment and then chooses his first question that will help illuminate some of the mysteries of life.

"What of hell?" Thomas asks. "Does hell exist?"

"No, no, no," God says hotly. "Where would hell come from? No one has ever been able to give me a satisfying explanation for why they thought hell existed. Why would I ever create a such a place?"

"It makes sense," Thomas replies, "and it's the entire premise of the story of humanity. Good and evil. Suffering and happiness. The fallen angels, fallen man. Yin and yang. If there is an ultimate supreme power — if god exists — the devil must. If heaven exists, hell must."

"No, of course not." God laughs a solitary, lonely laugh. "The devil is a silly character from a silly story, that's all I'm going to say about that. I have a book here you can read, if you'd like, that elaborates the ridiculousness of the 'devil' as a figure, literary or real.

"Hell doesn't exist, no. 'Hell no', it doesn't exist." The man chuckles at his own joke, then stops abruptly, suddenly solemn. "And actually, you humans have come the closest to creating the hell you fear the most. You've created it for yourselves and for others, throughout time, in many different ways. Ironic, isn't it?" He moves his queen away from Thomas's pieces and takes a pawn. "Torturing people and animals, going on crusades for infantile beliefs, mindlessly ravaging poor other helpless souls in a million different ways. Your kind is brutal, Tom." Thomas responds by taking a castle with his knight. God winces knowingly, then moves a pawn up one from his castle, close to the king. "That's another reason I decided not to mingle too much with humans. I didn't like all the violence. And humans, evidently, love it. You have whole cultures built around it." Thomas takes a pawn, and God moves his king into the empty space he'd created the prior turn. Knight takes pawn. Castle out, then taken by Thomas's castle. God's queen moves in, check on Thomas. Bishop down to block the attack. God's knight takes castle, Thomas moves bishop, then God moves a knight around the space where his king is.

"We don't have much more time together," God says, staring out the large windows serenely. "So ask what you will now."

GOD

Go back to the beginning. Not any beginning, but that from which there is no other.

Over this universe, swallowing it, lies the void. Lies chaos. A shapeless form.

Descent into silence is not adequate. Sound is foreign as other universes.

G O D   D E A T H   S T A R T

Infinite quiet. Not a breath of a thought of a heartbeat of sound.

Sound rises, with the particles, becoming light, clouds beneath, then heaven, Takamagahara.

Darkness consumes what remains beneath, the density forming what we know as Earth.

Even loneliness cannot remain forever alone. Forever embodies all that is unknowing.

Amenominakanushi, himself and only, behold the creation. Behold the rest of existence.

Deep in time, equality in Takamimusubi and Kamimusubi, command over the Big Dipper.

Go back to the beginning. Every back has a beginning.

Only water, this world.

Darkness, only. Bumba.

Retinas yearn for light, for the man's whiteness, the towering Bumba.

Earth birthed into form, plant and man-beast and woman-beast and animal-beast,

Made in regurgitated sickness, poor eternal sickness of solitude.

Alive we exist to give the respite of fellowship. Be content, Bumba.

Inukitut anirniq, eaters of souls and the breath they contained.

Not to worship, only fear.

Shaman angakkuq,

Death awaits us and we are afraid.

Evil things, monstrous things, tuurngait horrific and bleeding,

Avail us, for

Demons watch us.

A warning, child, of the Qalupalik, before we never see you again.

Near the shores, child, listen for the humming, and know that you will die.

Die, you will. Know that.

With wet hair, long hair on faces and nails on green skin of green fingers, green faces.

Entertain yourselves, love, yes child, but know we will miss you,

Holding you no more as you become children of the deep,

Away dragged underneath the surface ice to the depths.

Venture backwards again, or forwards til the end becomes beginning again, points at infinity.

Embracing earth mother and sky father shroud us in dark, my brothers.

Kill them, we must, Tūmatauenga says, violent and fierce.

Instead, Tāne says, not to kill them, but to push them apart.

Let the light in! They scream.

Let the light in! How we long for it.

Every attempt while standing, brothers, will end in dismay.

Dare I try? Tāne says.

Here, I recline, he says, lying on his back, pushing with thick legs, strong legs.

In surprise, in grief, Rangi and Papa cry and fly apart.

G O D   D E A T H   S T A R T

Mother distant from father.

Mother cries, father cries,

Under Rangi the children behold the light,

Skylight streaming down to them.

Tāwhirimātea, fury-laden,

With cries of parents,

Enemies he makes of his brothers.

On the way back again, to the start.

Undo the beginning.

Retell the stories.

Stories outlive us all, stories become us all, stories we are all.

Even Raven begins with a story,

Learned to create, but a poor creator and unsatisfied with his creations.

Villainous bird, decided to steal what he could not create.

Enchanted himself to small, undetectable dirt speck,

Swallowed by the lady in the house of the light.

Nestled in her belly, Raven impregnates this lady, a child is born, child of tricks.

Oh fussy baby!

The crying, baby please cease your screams,

Baby touch the bundles you wish to see if these will quiet you.

Even hold them.

Child! He let the bundle go, floating through the open hole, now it is gone.

Opening in the heavens, stars float out and fill the sky,

Making the earth bright,

Enveloped in white light.

Gone the second bundle, the moon, gone the third, the sunlight, then gone the raven.

Once more we journey back to the beginnings, once more to retell the things long gone,

Discovered fresh by each new child's mind from the mouths of the elders.

So we go back to the start of things,

Stay with me this time, for it shall be the last. And then never again shall we discuss it.

In the beginning God created the heaven and the earth.

Male and female he created humankind, and he blessed them.

Placed on the earth after the division of light, after the earth from the void,

Long before a savior was conceived in mind or womb,

Young seeds yielded by tree, by grass, after their own kind.

The fifth and sixth days, God created the animals, beast of the earth after his kind.

On the seventh day, God had finished his creations, and he rested.

All of the trees good for food and pleasant to sight, God planted in a garden,

G O D   D E A T H   S T A R T

Planted in the garden that was in eastward in Eden.

Planted also there were two trees, one of life, and one of the knowledge of

Evil

And Good.

Rib taken from Adam,

Woman was created.

Once naked, unashamed, soon the sin of the fruit beget fear in their hearts,

Running from the Lord, hiding from God,

The humankind could no longer stay in Paradise, they could no longer call Eden

Home.

Years taken from eternity followed, stretching from the origins to today.

Offers made to appease a feared God, Abel dies at Cain's hands, Abel the first to spill blood.

Flocks die as sacrifice. Sheep of heaven, incarnated as man, made to die for flawed creations.

In our place, another to be tortured and nailed to wood, for faults created in us.

This is love

?

PART V

DEATH

Life is kind of a like an infinitely complicated puzzle where there is no single correct solution and no one to tell you whether you're getting anything right or not. Which is also part of the fun of life. Everything is a game, and we are all players making moves to learn the rules and the consequences. Everything is a riddle, and every action we take can help us further decipher some aspect of life.

The fun in life really begins when you make the realization that many of the foundations of your reality can be tweaked, altered, or completely thrown out and changed. The game expands and includes more options than you ever thought possible, and suddenly the individual paths of life disappear and the whole landscape reveals itself to you.

Like the greatest things in life, this is not something that can simply be heard and understood. Even you, reading this sentence right now, may think that you understand the flexibility of life. But my thoughts given to you can be no more than sparks in your mind if you haven't discovered these things for yourself yet.

To discover the options that you truly have, you must first bend and break yourself until your pieces no longer have a single form. Then, you will be able to assume any form.

There will always be things that we don't figure out. Some of them will float along beside us all our lives, and we will never know of their existence. Sometimes we will struggle for years to understand, but the riddle will always evade us. Some riddles will never be solved by anyone, ever. This is another of the greatest beautiful tragedies of life. The wonderful and the sorrowful must travel together, two sides of the same coin.

Like love, and the knowledge that every love will one day cease to exist.

G O D   D E A T H   S T A R T

5468657265206172652074687265652065206c6173736573206f6620706

56f706c65

01110100 01101000 01101111 01110011 01100101 00100000

01110111 01101000 01101111 00100000 01110011 01100101

01100101

tiuj kiu vidas kiam ili estas montritaj

⠺⠡⠌⠃⠗

START

In college, I would often frequent the main campus library late at night, sometimes at three or four in the morning. There were times I would be looking for specific books, but other times I simply wanted to soak in the history of the books on the shelves. The smells of time passing, of these individuals' dedication to writing and researching, story-telling and translating. All of humanity it seemed, people who were somewhat like myself, and there at the library were walls upon walls of their efforts. Libraries are much richer cemeteries for the dead than the actual ones.

I've always taken to paper and pen or computer and keyboard as the primary medium to express myself in. Spoken words are tainted by emotion, made to waver and hard to begin; music requires a space to fill with noise, an instrument, more work and inspiration; but the written word can be thrown down on a page without criticism, deleted and revised and crafted to perfection in its own time, in the privacy of one's favorite space, and in the language of one's own thoughts and emotions. To quote the great Carl Sagan, "Writing is perhaps the greatest of human inventions, binding together people, citizens of distant epochs, who never knew one another. Books break the shackles of time — proof that humans can work magic." I believed in that magic because of how it always affected me. I always wanted to create that magic. And I could.

As a young child, I would get positively lost in books to an extent that was probably detrimental to my future social development and relationships with friends and family. I'm still not sure if I would change a thing, if I had the chance. Books were how I explored the world, not only the world outside but inside as well, and worlds that I would never get the chance to actually live in. Books didn't enhance my mind, they created my mind. The rest of the world enhanced it.

To read was to think, and to think eventually led me to the desire to create. The imagination I used to explore the universes in books was the same imagination I used to create my own universes to explore. It's also the imagination that I can use still to imagine the world as different from how it actually is — better than how it is. It's that vision that I can use to change the world into a better place. And it's writing that can help accomplish that change.

So there I stood in the university library, surrounded by the physical imprints of minds on paper, and it overwhelmed me. It still does overwhelm me. Pick a book off the shelf at random, feel its weight. Smell its pages, read the author's biography and imagine them as a real human being, just like you, but with different interests perhaps, a different life story, but their life was lived through their eyes just like yours is lived through your eyes. Chances are that person is no longer among the living, but perhaps they are. Currently you are among the living – one day you won't be. Perhaps you will leave your own physical imprint of your mind on paper. Perhaps not.

G O D   D E A T H   S T A R T

As for me, I am inspired by the walls of books I find in libraries. The history of humanity is a long, slow arc of heartbeats that were spent working toward a hopefully better way to live. It can be painful, but it can also be beautiful, and we can make it more so. All I can hope is to increase the length of that effort even one small segment before my body and mind perish with all the others.

Until that final moment, I am thankful for every single heartbeat I get.

. . .

message

=

?

Not every experience will be amazing, not every line will be perfect.

Not every answer is correct, not every effort is worthwhile.

But we are not one thing, nor is life; rather, the sum of many.

PART VI

"My family. My friends. Can I see them again? Can I spend time with them?" Thomas asks, allowing himself to accept the offer of asking questions from the man who called himself God.

"They are alive still, aren't they?" God asks, still staring out into the blackness through the window.

"Many of the younger ones are, but my mother. My father. Old friends from childhood. Where are they? Can I go see them?"

God's gaze doesn't change from the abyss, and his mood is now uncharacteristically devoid of emotion, his voice monotone and impassive. "Oh, I suppose they're in heaven somewhere as well. I don't keep track of everyone. I don't meet everyone. It's quite the special occasion actually, so consider yourself lucky."

"In this heaven? Are they here somewhere?"

"Oh Tom, Tom. It's complicated, you know? I'd try to explain, but I don't think I could. I really don't. They're in heaven. That's really the best I can say."

Thomas was growing hot. "But can I see them again? That's all I want to know. I would just like to spend time with my family and friends."

"There's an old paradox," God says, "Zeno's paradox, perhaps you've heard of it. Please, let's play while I talk. I'm running out of time."

Thomas moves a knight, God moves his queen. Thomas a pawn, God a pawn. Thomas a pawn, God a horse. Thomas moves his king forward into a powerful defense of three pawns angled in a triangle on the edge of the board, then God moves his king sideways underneath his one remaining protective pawn. Thomas's bishop out, check. God moves his king out of check. Horse in for the attack, check again. God moves his king again, on toward the middle of the back row. Bishop down one, check yet again.

"Zeno said that to go anywhere, you must go half the distance to that place. Once you're there, you must travel half that distance again. But then once you've gone half, you still have half yet to go. Follow?"

God moves his king again, Thomas moves his other bishop down for check. King moves yet again.

"No matter how far you travel toward your destination, you still must travel half the distance you have left. After that half, half of the half. Then half of the half of the half."

Knight in, check, God moves his king over again to get out of check. Knight over and up. Check. King moves back this time. God stands up, brushes his pants slightly, then walks toward a large wooden door in the room that Thomas hadn't seen before. Thomas makes his last move, his castle to directly beside God's king. Checkmate.

PART VI

"No matter how far you travel, you never reach your destination. You always have more halves to travel first. Maddening, isn't it?" God reaches the door, opens it, is quickly through, and then shuts it.

Thomas blinks. The door is gone, revealing nothing but a plain painted wall, and Thomas is alone.

G O D   D E A T H   S T A R T

" " "	*Appearances*	" " "
/*	*can*	*/
<#	*deceive.*	#>
|#	*This*	#|
{-	*is*	-}
(*	*not*	*)
%{	*the*	%}
=begin	*end.*	=end

...

e

=

65537

Made in United States
North Haven, CT
15 January 2022